Please return or renew this item by the last date shown. There may be a charge if you fail to do so. Items can be returned to any Westminster library.

Telephone: Enquiries 020 7641 1300
Renewals (24 hour service) 020 7641 1400
Online renewal service available.
Web site: www.westminster.gov.uk

For Romilly Deal

Special thanks to Valerie Wilding

ORCHARD BOOKS

First published in Great Britain in 2021 by The Watts Publishing Group

1 3 5 7 9 10 8 6 4 2

Text copyright © 2021 Working Partners Limited
Illustrations © Orchard Books 2021
Series created by Working Partners Limited

A CIP catalogue record for this book is available from the British Library.

ISBN 978 1 40836 194 8

Printed and bound in Great Britain by Clays Ltd, Elcograf S.p.A.

The paper and board used in this book are made from wood from responsible sources.

Orchard Books
An imprint of Hachette Children's Group
Part of The Watts Publishing Group Limited
Carmelite House
50 Victoria Embankment
London EC4Y 0DZ

An Hachette UK Company

www.hachette.co.uk
www.hachettechildrens.co.uk

Contents

Meet the Characters

Aisha and Emily are best friends from Spellford Village. Aisha loves sports, whilst Emily's favourite thing is science. But what both girls enjoy more than anything is visiting Enchanted Valley and helping their unicorn friends, who live there.

Quickhoof

The four Sports and Games Unicorns help to make games and competitions fun for everyone. Quickhoof uses her magic locket to help players work well as a team.

Feeling confident in your skills and abilities is so important for sporting success. Brightblaze's magic helps to make sure everyone believes in themselves!

Brightblaze

Fairtail

Games are no fun when players cheat or don't follow the rules. Fairtail's magic locket reminds everyone to play fair!

When things get difficult, Spiritmane's perseverance locket gives sportspeople the strength to face their challenges and succeed.

Spiritmane

Enchanted Cottage

← Golden Palace

An Enchanted Valley lies a twinkle away,
Where beautiful unicorns live, laugh and play
You can visit the mermaids, or go for a ride,
So much fun to be had, but dangers can hide!

Your friends need your help – this is how you know:
A keyring lights up with a magical glow.
Whirled off like a dream, you won't want to leave.
Friendship forever, when you truly believe.

Chapter One
Bawling Billy and Weeping Whiskerina

Aisha Khan looked at the board game boxes spread over the sitting-room floor. She sat with her best friend Emily Turner.

"Which shall we play?" she asked.

Emily laughed. "It's too hard to decide. I want to play them all!"

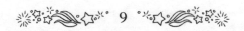

They had planned to practise skateboarding together after lunch, but it was pouring with rain, so Emily had raced over to Aisha's house – Enchanted Cottage – with her jacket over her head. Now they were trying to choose a game.

"What about Greedy Goat?" said Aisha, holding up a farm-themed board game. "That was really fun last time!"

But Emily wasn't listening. She was pointing to the crystal unicorn keyring that was clipped to Aisha's belt.

"It's glowing!" said Emily. She pulled a matching keyring from her pocket. "Mine's glowing, too!"

Aisha's eyes sparkled. "Hooray! Queen Aurora's calling us! We'll see all our friends again."

Soon after the Khans had moved to Enchanted Cottage, Aisha and Emily found themselves transported to Enchanted Valley. This was a wonderful land of unicorns and other fantastic creatures, ruled by the kind and gentle unicorn, Queen Aurora. After their first adventure, they were given two magical keyrings. These keyrings were what they used to get back to the valley.

Emily grinned. "A magical adventure would be just the thing to brighten up a wet day!" she said.

The girls held out their keyrings and felt them being pulled together, as if by a strong magnet. When the unicorns' horns touched, a flurry of dazzling colours surrounded Emily and Aisha. Blue, indigo, pink and green sparkles whirled around them, faster and faster. The girls felt their feet lift right off the carpet as they were swept into the magical swirl.

Excitement fizzed through them. They were off to Enchanted Valley!

Moments later, the sparkles began to fade. Aisha and Emily felt their feet touch the ground once more. When the sparkles cleared they found themselves standing on rich green grass at the foot of a familiar hill. At the top was Queen Aurora's glittering golden palace, topped with twisting turrets shaped like unicorn horns.

Nearby was the stunning silver sports

stadium the girls had seen on their recent adventures. Sunlight glinted off its silvery walls, and brilliantly coloured flags fluttered high above from tall, twisty poles.

Aisha and Emily knew that the Enchanted Valley Games were due to be held there soon. They hugged each other.

"Isn't it great to be back?" said Emily.

Aisha pointed to the palace. A beautiful unicorn was trotting over the silver drawbridge. "Here comes Queen Aurora!" she said.

The unicorn's golden mane and tail glittered and sparkled, and her coat shimmered like a summer dawn: pink, yellow, soft red and orange. She wore a silver crown and her golden horn gleamed brightly in the sunshine.

Four other unicorns followed the
queen. The girls recognised them as their
friends, the Sports and Games Unicorns.

Emily and Aisha smiled. "Hello, Queen
Aurora! Hello, everyone!"

"Welcome back," Aurora said in her soft,
musical voice.

Quickhoof, the buttercup-yellow Teamwork unicorn, and Brightblaze, the scarlet-maned Confidence unicorn, dipped their horns in greeting and said, "Hello!"

"It's lovely to see you again," said Emily.

Aisha stroked Spiritmane's soft lavender neck. "I see you haven't got your locket back yet," she said.

All the Enchanted Valley unicorns wore a magical locket that protected something important to everyone who lived there. Spiritmane took care of Perseverance, which meant never giving up.

Spiritmane shook her head. "I haven't. Nor has Fairtail," she said, glancing over at the sea-green unicorn, who looked after Sportsmanship.

Queen Aurora said sadly, "I'm afraid Selena still has them."

Selena was an evil unicorn. She'd stolen the lockets from all the Sports and Games Unicorns. Aisha and Emily, with help from their friends, had managed to get two lockets back, but Selena still had the others. She was refusing to give them up unless she was made queen of Enchanted Valley.

There was no way Aisha and Emily were going to let that happen. Selena didn't care about peace and friendship. She would ruin everything!

Fairtail hung her head. "Without my locket nobody will play or compete

fairly," she said.

"That's right, so starting the Games without it would be hopeless," said Queen Aurora. "We're having serious problems right now. Come and see."

She turned towards the shining silver stadium. Aisha and Emily followed, but before they'd gone far, they heard someone crying.

The girls peeped behind a cluster of sweet-smelling dinglebell flowers, and saw a fluffy white bunny. He wore green and white striped shorts, and had enormous blue eyes and silky whiskers.

"A baby pufflebunny!" said Emily.

"And a kitterfly!" said Aisha. A pale gold kitten's lemon-yellow wings flapped as she bounced up and down, looking very cross.

Both creatures were in tears.

"What's wrong?" asked Emily.

The pufflebunny pointed a furry paw at the kitterfly. "We had a go-kart race and Whiskerina cheated! She sent me the wrong way around the Sleeping Willow tree, then called me a loser. She's a cheat!"

Whiskerina's wings flapped so hard she rose off the ground. "I didn't cheat, Billy!"

"You did!" said the pufflebunny.

Aisha patted his quivering paw. "I don't expect she meant to cheat," she said.

Whiskerina dabbed her eyes with a wingtip. "I didn't," she said. "I never cheat." She sniffed, then she sighed. "Well,

not normally ... but I did today, I admit."

Now Billy and Whiskerina were calmer, Aisha and Emily went to where Queen Aurora was quietly watching with Fairtail.

"You see?" Aurora said. "Without Fairtail's Sportsmanship locket, they can't play fairly."

"And it isn't just the Games it will spoil," Fairtail added. "Nobody will be able to play fairly at anything so it will ruin the whole valley!"

Aurora's mane shimmered as she shook her head. "This will only get worse," she said, "but we must have peace in Enchanted Valley."

Aisha swallowed hard. "Are ... are you

saying the only option is to give in to Selena? To give her your crown and make her queen?"

"That's awful!" cried Emily.

Fairtail glanced at Aurora, then said, "We do have a plan to get my locket back, but we can't do it alone. Emily and Aisha, will you help?"

The girls were thrilled. "Of course we will!"

Chapter Two
Boardway Park Board Games

Emily and Aisha clambered on to a low, thick branch of a sweetbark tree, and listened as Queen Aurora explained the plan.

"We'll do a practice run-through of part of the Games," she said. "It's the Board Games Tournament."

Emily and Aisha looked at her in surprise.

"Board games?" said Emily. "In a sporting event?"

"Of course! Board games are just as important and fun to play as sports," said Aurora. "Besides," she added, with a twinkle in her eyes, "these are Enchanted Valley board games. They're probably different from the ones you play at home!"

Aisha and Emily squeezed each other's hands. This sounded exciting!

"How will the plan work?" asked Aisha.

Aurora trotted closer and said quietly, "We hope Selena won't realise it's a practice. If she thinks it's a real game,

she'll want to ruin it. That will give us a chance to get Fairtail's locket back!"

"It's a great plan!" said Emily. "Let's do it!"

Queen Aurora had to go and protect her palace in case Selena tried any nasty tricks to get inside. Brightbold, Quickhoof and Spiritmane stayed to comfort the pufflebunny and kitterfly.

"Jump on my back," Fairtail said. "We'll fly to Boardway Park."

Aisha and Emily adored flying and loved seeing new parts of Enchanted Valley! They stood on the branch and climbed on to the unicorn's back. Emily buried her hands in Fairtail's mane, which sparkled like the ocean. Aisha sat behind with her arms around her friend.

Fairtail leapt into the air. The wind made Emily catch her breath, and she heard Aisha laughing behind her. Emily's fair hair was blowing into Aisha's face, tickling her nose and making her giggle.

As they soared above Enchanted Valley, cross, shouty voices floated up to them. Just below, they were able to make out one, two, three … four! flying pink piggles playing hide-and-seek in the clouds. They looked just like pigs, but they could hover through the air, leaving trails of sparkles behind them.

"Found you, Gigglegrunt!" said the seeker.

Gigglegrunt flew out from behind a

small puff of cloud, looking furious. "You cheated, Twinkletrot! You peeked as you counted!"

"Did not!" said Twinkletrot.

"You did!"

"I didn't mean to. I couldn't help it!" squeaked Twinkletrot.

"Oh dear!" Emily said, her excitement leaving as quickly as it had arrived.

"We must get the locket back, or everyone will cheat at everything!" Aisha cried.

Moments later, Fairtail called, "There's Boardway Park." She swooped down and circled over a clearing. There was a play area with swings and roundabouts of different sizes, but nobody was using it.

Instead, elves, goblins and other creatures were clustered around little tables and chairs. One goblin seemed to be dancing on the daisy-speckled grass. The girls realised he was trying not to tread on a lively group of tiny white birds.

"They're quacklets," Fairtail said as she landed. "If they're not dancing, they're hopping and if they're not hopping, they're playing chase-my-tail!"

The quacklets broke into a fierce, squeaky squabble. The only word Aisha could make out was, "Cheat!"

"Oh dear," she said. "There's no sportsmanship here, either."

An elf tipped over a game board and threw the playing pieces around. He was so cross that his pointed ears turned bright red.

"I didn't cheat," sobbed his friend.

Aisha sighed. "We *really* need that locket."

Fairtail tossed her head. "Here's someone to help us," she said. "It's Buckle the leprechaun. He's the Board Games Master and we've already told him the plan."

A little man in a green suit walked over, swinging his walking stick. He had a ginger beard, and buckles shimmered on his boots, his belt, and even on his green top hat. Even wearing his tall hat he only reached up to the girls' shoulders.

"Ah, Fairtail's brought two smiley

friends!" said Buckle. "That's grand!"

The unicorn introduced the girls, and explained about them helping Queen Aurora.

"That's kind," said Buckle. "Well, Emily and Aisha, I'm in charge of the Boardway

Park games. So let's get started!"

He held the crooked handle of his stick in front of his mouth. "Board game players, gather round." Buckle's voice boomed, his stick working like a megaphone.

A pixie flew over. She had masses of purple curls stuffed under a fluffy nightcap.

"It's Trixie the sleep pixie!" cried Aisha. The girls had met her on a previous adventure.

"Hello, Trixie," said Emily, as the pixie hugged them in turn.

Trixie's nightie had a picture on the front of sleepy lambs jumping over a gate. She looked at the girls with wide purple eyes. "It's lovely to see you again," she said. "I'm playing, too, and so is Hob."

Aisha and Emily turned to see a goblin with a wrinkly green face, who was even smaller than Buckle.

"Hello, Hob!" they called.

The goblin swept off his pointy hat and bowed. His spectacles fell off, but a beautiful phoenix with a crest of orange feathers bent her head to pick them up. Six phoenix chicks clustered around her feet.

"Thanks, Ember," said Hob. "Are you playing?"

"Yes," said the phoenix. She fanned out her flame-like tail. "My chicks have come to see the start."

Emily bent down to the baby phoenixes.
"Have you come to cheer your mum on?"
she asked.

"Yes!" trilled the six. They stood in
a row, wingtip to wingtip. Their tails
swayed from side to side as they chanted.

"Our mum's a win-ner!"

Buckle opened a green box. Inside were some large yellow dice, a pack of circular cards and a folded game board. The playing pieces were top hats, like the leprechaun's, but in different colours. Buckle took out the game board and, with a flick of his wrist, unfolded it.

"Wow!" said Aisha. "It looks just like Enchanted Valley!"

As she spoke, tiny models sprang up on the board. *Pop! Pop! Pop!* There was the queen's palace, the silver stadium and the Pufflebunny Inn.

A glow appeared in the middle of the board.

"What's happening?" cried Emily.

The glow grew into a tall column of brilliant light.

"Wow!" said Aisha.

"Keep watching ..." Buckle said.

The dazzling beam grew as high as a pine

tree, then burst into a great fountain of light. It shone all over the valley, as far as the girls could see.

Emily stared. "What's happened?" she asked, hoping it was something wonderful.

"That magic fountain of light turned the whole of Enchanted Valley into a huge game board," Buckle told her. "That's where you'll be playing!"

The girls were thrilled. This was better than any game they'd ever played before!

The leprechaun tossed a yellow die into the air. It hovered beside him!

"There are no numbers on it," Emily whispered.

"That's strange," Aisha replied. "I

wonder how it works?"

Buckle explained the game as he put the board away. "When you throw the die, you'll learn what to do," he said. "As you travel around the board, collect as many rings as you can find. You'll need the rings at the end of the game. But," he said, looking around at the players, "be careful not to collect the reset ring. That will send you back to the beginning!"

Emily nudged Aisha. "We must remember that."

"What about rules?" asked Hob.

"Ah, the rules, to be sure," said Buckle. "Hmm … Fairtail usually uses her Sportsmanship locket to magically set the rules. She hasn't got her locket, but she'll

still explain them, won't you, Fairtail?"

"Gladly!" said the unicorn. "Rule One: take turns to roll the die. Rule Two: no taking shortcuts. Rule Three: no cheating. This one is very important. Players who cheat will be disqualified."

Everyone was excited! Ember's wings twitched, and Hob hopped from one foot to the other. Trixie whizzed around so fast her nightcap flew off, and Fairtail's horn sent out tiny crackling sparks!

The girls could hardly wait!

"It's going to be such fun," said Emily.

"Yes," said Aisha, "but let's remember we're doing this to lure that horrible Selena here. Then we'll have a chance to get Fairtail's locket back."

Just then, lightning streaked across the blue sky, followed by a crash of thunder.

Buckle held on to his top hat. "Wh-what … ?"

Aisha and Emily looked up. A silver unicorn loomed high above them. Her deep blue mane and tail waved wildly and her purple eyes blazed. Sparking hooves crackled as they pawed the air.

"Selena!" cried Emily.

Chapter Three
Top Hats and Dice

Even though this was exactly what they'd planned – that their practice game would make Selena appear – the girls couldn't help feeling scared.

Aisha glanced at Buckle and Fairtail. The leprechaun had turned pale, and the unicorn was tossing her head uneasily.

As Selena flew lower, the girls realised that someone they knew was running over to greet her.

"It's Grubb the ogre!" said Emily, in dismay.

When Selena landed, Grubb tumbled over to her. As he scrambled along, his lumpy cheeks wobbled and his flabby ears flapped back and forth.

Trixie, Hob and Ember edged back, but Fairtail and the girls stood their ground.

"Ah, the two silly girls," said Selena, "and the useless unicorn who couldn't keep hold of her locket."

"That's because you stole it," said Fairtail. "Where is it?"

The evil unicorn cackled. "Look at Grubb."

The Sportsmanship locket dangled from the ogre's thick, hairy neck. He laughed. "Geh! Geh!"

"You'll never get the locket back,"

sneered Selena.

"We will," Emily said quietly.

"Ha!" said Selena. "This stupid board game will be a disaster. I'll soon be laughing at all you losers! Grubb?"

The tufty bristles that sprouted from the ogre's chin twitched. "Yes, Your Highness," he said.

"You're going to play with these silly creatures," said Selena. "And because you've got the Sportsmanship locket, you can change the rules."

"Awesome!" said Grubb.

Emily glanced at Aisha. "I don't like the sound of that," she whispered.

Selena's eyes flashed. "Grubb's new rule," she said, "is that no one can cheat …"

The girls shared a confused glance. *This doesn't sound like Selena*, thought Aisha.

"No one can cheat," Selena continued, "except Grubb. *He* can cheat as much as he likes."

Before anyone could argue, she reared up and flew off, cackling.

Grubb strutted around, looking pleased with himself. "Check out *my* locket!" he said, pointing to where the locket lay on his chest.

Aisha glared at him. "It's *not* your locket, and you know it," she said. "Give it back to Fairtail!"

Grubb scowled. "No way. I never win anything, but that's all about to change now." He laughed. "No one cheats ... No one except *me*!"

Emily turned to Fairtail. "He can't do this!"

But the unicorn said sadly, "He can, with the power of my Sportsmanship locket."

Aisha frowned. "Fine! But he won't have it for long."

"We'll make sure of that!" Emily added.

Buckle looked quite shaken by seeing Selena. He tried to plaster on an encouraging smile. "Ahem … I'd better start the game."

He clapped once. The air in front of him shimmered like sparkling mist. It cleared to reveal a large silver trophy. It was shaped like a bowl supported by three

unicorn horns, and it
turned slowly in
mid-air.

The ogre
rubbed his
grimy hands
together.
"There's my
prize."

"Not yet!"
said Aisha.

"Not ever, if
we can help it!" Emily
added.

"Ahem," said Buckle. "The trophy
will be magically hidden somewhere in
Enchanted Valley. The only way to find it

is to complete the game. Whoever touches it first will be the winner."

"*My* prize," Grubb said again.

Buckle ignored him. "Don't forget, collecting rings along the way will help you win," he said. "Sometimes you'll find them; sometimes you'll earn them by completing tasks."

He clapped again, and said,

"*Fly away, fly away.*

Cross the skies.

Wait for the winner

To claim their prize."

The trophy rose into the air. Just before it whooshed away, Grubb pulled the locket and chain over his head and hurled it into the bowl.

He gave a wonky grin. "Now the locket's safe. You stinky girls won't get it because you won't win."

The other players gathered around the girls. Aisha stroked Fairtail's sea-green neck, comforting her.

"What do we do?" asked Trixie.

Hob shrugged. "Play, of course."

Ember nodded. "If we don't play, we can't win."

"And we must win to get the locket back," said Aisha. "There are six of us, so we have six chances of winning. It doesn't matter who comes first, as long as it isn't Grubb. Agreed?"

Everyone nodded nervously. "Agreed!"

Buckle tossed a blue hat to Aisha. It

looked far too small, but as she put it on, it grew until it fitted her head perfectly.

"Your hat's glowing!" said Emily. She put a red one on.

Aisha helped Trixie to jam her yellow hat over her purple curls. Everyone laughed as the pixie's hat grew and grew, until almost all her hair was neatly tucked inside.

Fairtail's white hat even provided slots for her ears. Hob wasn't pleased about having to take his own hat off and wear a pink one.

"It's not pointy," he grumbled.

Grubb got an orange hat, which had to grow a hundred times its size to fit on his massive, lumpy head.

Once they were all wearing their brightly coloured hats, Buckle said, "You are the playing pieces now." He passed out maps. "These will help you find your way around."

Buckle stood back, but as Trixie and

Ember flapped their wings and left the ground, he shouted, "Stop! I almost forgot. No flying. Everyone must walk."

He patted the yellow die, and it bobbed towards Aisha. "Blue hat always starts a new game," he said. "That's why your hat's glowing – it's your turn."

Aisha held the die. "It's blank!" she said.

Buckle grinned and said, "Roll it." So she did.

When the die stopped, everyone was surprised to see it showed a picture!

"It's Flowerdew Garden!" said Emily. "We've been there."

"That's where your first task is," said Buckle. "Go, go, go!"

Grubb lumbered away, followed by

the girls and their friends. As they knew where Flowerdew Garden was, maybe they'd get there before Grubb.

After a moment, Emily cried, "Look! A golden ring!"

It was looped over a tall grass stalk. She ran to take it, but Grubb charged back and pushed her over so he could grab the ring himself.

"Ow!" Emily yelled. "You … you …"

"Cheat!" Aisha shouted, helping Emily up.

The ogre laughed. "I'm allowed to cheat!"

Fairtail sighed. "It's going to be hard to win this game."

Emily and Aisha's eyes met. Fairtail

was right. But if they didn't win, they'd never get the locket back, and no one in Enchanted Valley would ever play fair again. They had very little chance of winning … but they had to do whatever they could to stop Grubb, or else Selena would become queen of Enchanted Valley.

Chapter Four
The Big Flower Challenge

As Aisha and Emily ran down a grassy slope, they spotted little pink clouds popping up from behind a copse of hazelnut trees.

"What's that?" asked Aisha.

The crest on top of Ember's head wobbled as she scurried along. "Mist from the Puffing Lily!" she said. "It only grows in Flowerdew Garden!"

"Then we're nearly there!" cried Emily.

They circled the copse, and saw before them the magical garden, bright with colourful flowers and fruits. Fairtail had to skid to a stop when Buckle appeared in a shower of green sparkles.

Buckle waited until Grubb joined the group, then produced the circular game cards. He handed one to Aisha, saying, "This tells you what to do."

Aisha read it aloud.

"*The garden's full of magic plants*
With flowers small and tall.
One minute's all you have to find
The biggest one of all."

"Three rings for the winner!" Buckle added. "Ready? GO!"

The friends gathered together. "We must beat Grubb," Emily said, "so do your best!"

Fairtail cantered into the middle of the garden. Trixie flapped her wings and was about to leap into the air, when she clapped her tiny hand to her mouth. "Oops! I almost forgot – no flying!"

Ember dashed in a zigzag pattern, while Hob stomped around, peering left and right.

Aisha found a large yellow fluttercup, but Emily spotted an even larger one at the same time.

"You have it," said Emily, who had just

seen a biggonia smiling up from behind a patch of quietly ticking dandelion clocks.

The girls found Hob sitting beside Buckle. He was clutching a pom-pom carnation the size of a football. Grubb was searching nearby, grunting as his lumbering feet pounded the paths.

Fairtail trotted to Buckle with a parasol pansy that was as big as a frisbee. Then Ember hurtled towards the friends with an enormous silvery flower clamped in her beak.

"A giant moonflower!" said Hob.

"Wow! That's the winner!" said Aisha, but just then, Grubb thundered over and snatched the moonflower from Ember.

"Cheat!" cried Emily.

Hob clutched her arm. "It doesn't matter – look!" he said.

Trixie raced towards them, carrying the biggest sunpower flower anyone had ever seen. Emily reckoned it was as big as the largest family-sized pizza.

"Yay, Trixie! That's a whopper!" yelled Aisha.

Buckle checked his watch. "Five seconds … four … three …"

"There!" said Trixie,

shoving the sunpower flower into the leprechaun's hand.

But as the friends cheered, Trixie's yellow top hat flew off and disappeared into the sky.

"Oh dear," said Buckle. "I'm sorry, but that means Trixie's disqualified. She cheated."

"No!" said Emily. "She wouldn't."

Trixie burst into loud sobs. "I did! I did! I'm sorry!" She wept. "I watered the sunpower flower with the gnomes' magic blooming-can so that it would grow ginormous. I'm so sorry. I don't know why I did it!"

Aisha gently cuddled the weeping pixie. "It was the stolen locket that made you

do it," she said.

"As I'm not wearing the locket," added Fairtail, "everyone will cheat sooner or later."

"Trixie, we know you're not really a cheater," said Emily. "Not like Grubb."

The ogre danced a clumsy jig. "Ha! I'm the winner! I get the rings!"

Buckle sighed sadly and said, "Even though Grubb cheated when he stole Ember's flower, he still gets three rings, because he's allowed to cheat." He tapped his hat buckle, and three golden rings flew into Grubb's filthy outstretched hand.

Emily put her hands on her hips in frustration. Aisha frowned.

It was the ogre's turn to throw the die.

He tossed it into a clump of Giggling Grass right by his feet, so nobody else could see it. He bent to look at the location it showed, then charged off.

"Cheat!" Aisha shouted.

"He's got a head start," grumbled Hob.

Emily wasted no time and peered at the dice. She saw a picture of an old oak tree. "Hob! It's your home! Hurry!"

The die floated back to Buckle, and Hob led the friends along a narrow path. "Here's a short cut," he cried. "This way!" He turned off the path and dived between the trees.

"Stop!" Fairtail cried, but she was too late. Hob's pink top hat whipped off his head and disappeared.

The girls stared.

"Of course!" said Emily. "Taking a short cut is cheating. Now Hob's out of the game as well as Trixie."

"I'm sorry!" the goblin said, looking miserable.

"Don't worry," Aisha said kindly. "There are still four of us left." She turned to the others. "Come on! We can still beat Grubb! *And* get that locket."

But with each round, it was looking less and less likely.

Chapter Five
Quickie Pix

The four remaining friends used the map to find their way to Hob's house. As they followed a trail lined with pink daisies that smelled of strawberry ice cream, they came across two squabbling little goblins outside a thatched cottage.

"You told Mum you swept the floor

properly," said one. "You cheated. You brushed the dirt under the rug."

"Didn't!"

"You did!"

Aisha shook her head crossly. "If you had your locket you'd put this right in a twinkling."

Fairtail sighed. "If I had my locket, this never would have happened in the first place!"

Aisha stroked the unicorn's mane. "We'll soon get it back," she said.

I hope so, Emily thought. She spotted a golden ring dangling from a twig. "Hooray! Another one," she said, tucking it in her pocket.

As they drew near to Hob's home, they

passed a young turtle who was crying quietly as his mum told him off.

"Don't ask your sister to do your fishtory homework," she said. "That's cheating!"

"I didn't mean to," the turtle said with a gulp. "It just came out."

The girls wished they could stop to comfort him, but finding the locket was more important.

Hob's home was reached through a gap in a thick tree trunk. They went inside, down a spiral staircase, through a tunnel into a large cavern. This was Hob's potion workshop. Crystal lights glittered on jars and bottles full of curious ingredients, stacked around his wonky shelves. Buckle was waiting, and Grubb was flopped on a squishy armchair that was far too small for him. It was *very* squished.

"Next is a drawing challenge, called Quickie Pix," Buckle announced. "You'll be in two teams."

Aisha whispered to Emily, "This sounds fun. You're good at drawing and I'm not bad. We'll make a great team!"

Buckle continued. "Aisha will team up with Ember. The other team will be Emily, Fairtail and Grubb."

The girls looked at each other. That wasn't what they wanted.

"The first player of each team gets a card with the name of an object, which

they have to draw," Buckle explained. "They must not speak. If their teammates guess what the picture is, the person who draws earns two rings, and the guesser earns one."

Emily pulled Aisha and Fairtail aside. "I won't guess what Grubb draws. If I do, he'll get two gold rings."

Fairtail leaned close. "You must do your best to guess," she whispered. "If you don't, it's cheating, isn't it? You'll be disqualified."

Emily's heart sank. "I suppose so," she sighed. "I don't want to help Grubb, but I'll have to."

"Ready?" asked Buckle. He tapped his green top hat on the floor twice. Two whiteboards on easels sprang up, with marker pens hovering beside them.

Ember was first to draw for her team, and Grubb for his. Aisha sat on a floor cushion as the phoenix took the pen in her wingtip and drew a round shape, then added two legs. Aisha thought it could be a bird.

Meanwhile, Grubb clutched the pen in his dirty fist and began drawing. He

pressed so hard, Emily thought he might carve his picture in the board.

Aisha was sure Ember's picture was a bird. It had lots of tail feathers. She racked her brain for a bird with a fluffy tail. "Ostrich!" she shouted.

Ember shook her head.

"A parrot? A vulture?" Aisha tried.

Ember shook her head again and whispered a few words.

"Peacock!" Aisha shouted.

Immediately Ember's hat vanished. "No!" she cried. "I didn't say the answer. I just said, 'It likes showing off its tail.' I wasn't cheating."

Buckle said, "The rule is no speaking. I'm sorry, Ember, you're disqualified."

Meanwhile, Emily gave a quiet gasp. She'd guessed what Grubb had drawn. "Welly boot," she said in a flat voice.

Grubb nearly exploded with delight. "Two rings! Two rings!" he grunted, as they dropped into his hairy hand.

"Yes, Grubb, you won Quickie Pix,"
said Buckle sadly, "so you can throw the
die to select the final game."

The die floated to the ogre's hand. He
rolled it, and everyone bent to see where
to go next.

"It looks like trees with colourful
flowers," said Aisha. "Where's that?"

Grubb thundered along the tunnel and
up the stairs – he clearly knew.

"I think it's Flicker Thicket," Fairtail
said. "Let's go!"

They set off. Just outside Hob's home
Aisha found a gold ring. "Grubb was
in such a hurry he missed it," she said,
stuffing the ring in her pocket.

They followed Fairtail down a steep,

stony slope. When the unicorn suddenly stopped, the girls stumbled into her.

"What's up?" asked Emily.

"A ring!" said Fairtail, looking up to where a blue ring dangled from a thin, prickly branch. It was bigger than the gold rings.

"Maybe it counts for more," said Aisha. "Can you reach it?"

Fairtail reared up, and hooked the ring with her horn. As she dropped down, Buckle appeared in a flurry of crackling green sparkles, and the ring vanished.

Buckle shook his head. "Sorry, Fairtail. That was the Reset Ring. You must go back to the beginning again."

"Oh no!" the girls cried.

Fairtail's eyes filled with tears. "Girls, I'm so sorry. I wish I could help you beat Grubb!"

They hugged her velvety neck. "It's not your fault," Aisha said.

"Don't worry," Emily added. "We'll do our best."

"I know you will," said Fairtail. She walked away slowly, head down. "I'm sure you can win."

The girls looked at each other nervously.

"It's just us — to save Enchanted Valley," said Aisha.

"Two girls against an ogre," added Emily.

They didn't want to give up, but they had no idea how they could possibly win. Enchanted Valley would be lost for sure.

Chapter Six
Butterfly Ride

Flicker Thicket was a dense mound of shrubbery. In the centre of the mound grew a single tree with emerald green leaves. All the way up the trunk, the leaves were large and flat. They were dotted with pink and purple caterpillars, while dainty butterflies of every colour fluttered

among the branches.

Aisha caught her breath. "I've never seen such a beautiful tree!"

Emily stared. "And all those butterflies too. It's magical!"

A grunt echoed from the thicket. There stood Grubb, tapping his foot. Beside him was Buckle, not smiling.

Aisha glanced anxiously at Emily. "This is it," she said. "Our last chance. We must win if we're to get that locket."

"Ahem," said Buckle. "Your final challenge is a game of Caterpillars and Butterflies. Imagine the tree is the game board. The large flat leaves all the way up the trunk are like the spaces on the board. You roll the die to see how many spaces to move. Have you got that?"

"Yes," said the girls. Grubb grunted.

"Your goal is to get to the top of the tree," said the leprechaun, "and take the trophy."

The girls looked up. The silver trophy hovered just above the very topmost leaf of the tree.

"If you land on a leaf with a butterfly on," Buckle continued, "she will grow big enough to fly you to a higher leaf."

"Wow!" said Aisha and Emily, thrilled.

"If you land on a leaf with a caterpillar, you'll slide down his back to a lower leaf."

"I get it!" said Aisha. "It's like my Snakes and Ladders game at home, but with caterpillars instead of snakes, and

butterflies instead of ladders."

Buckle grinned. "Girls! Have you never played Caterpillars and Butterflies before?"

"Never," said Emily.

"Oh, that's good!" Buckle danced a little jig. "That means you get beginner's luck!"

With a flick of his wrist, he produced two four-leafed clovers, one for each of them.

"Ooh, these will give us a better chance of winning!" said Aisha. "Let's tuck them in our hair."

Grubb sneered. "Luck's no good when I can cheat!"

Buckle asked everyone to count their

rings. "That will tell you how many spaces you can move up the tree before this round starts," he explained.

The girls counted. Emily had seven, and Aisha six.

Grubb counted loudly so they could all hear. "Five, six, seven," he said. A moment

or two later, they heard him again. "Twenty-four, twenty-five, twenty-six ..."

"Hey!" Emily cried. "He's counting his over and over. Grubb, you've got more than us anyway, so why cheat?"

Grubb grinned, showing three grey-green teeth, and said, "Because I can."

Buckle checked how many rings everyone had. "You'll start halfway up the tree, Grubb," he said. "A butterfly will take you."

The ogre ran to jump on to a butterfly. She grew to a huge size, but still squeaked, "Ow!" as he landed on her back. She had to flap hard to carry Grubb to his starting point.

The girls were starting so low down the

trunk they could each easily clamber on to their first leaf.

"It's weird standing on these leaves," said Aisha. "They're very strong." The leaves didn't even waver as the girls hopped up.

Buckle called to the ogre. "Grubb, you won the last game, so you'll roll the die first." He held it out. It floated up until the ogre could snatch it out of the air. He rolled it.

"Four!" he said, and climbed up four spaces, landing on a leaf with a butterfly. He climbed on its back.

"Eek!" she said, and slowly managed to fly Grubb to a higher level.

He flung the die to Emily. She rolled a

three and was just about to step on a butterfly leaf when a thick twig crashed down, frightening the butterfly away before Emily reached it.

"Ha ha!" she heard Grubb laugh from above.

"He's enjoying himself, the cheat," Aisha said grimly. She rolled a six, and began climbing. Just before she reached

her leaf, all the butterflies fluttered up to where Grubb was tossing little golden bobbles around.

"Sorry, girls," Buckle called from below. "Butterflies can't resist honey buds."

Aisha and Emily sighed and gritted their teeth.

Grubb rolled the die and got a three. The girls counted spaces and grinned when they realised Grubb would land on a long caterpillar. But just before he did, he growled at the caterpillar, which immediately turned into a butterfly.

"Bully! Cheat!" shouted Emily.

Grubb carried on, cheating whenever he liked. But when the girls threw six after

six, and never landed on a caterpillar, they realised their beginner's luck was working. Soon they were level with the ogre.

As they drew near the treetop and the trophy, a beautiful bluebird with a silvery crest flew down and perched between them.

"I'll help you beat that horrible cheat," she trilled softly. "I'll ask a caterpillar to take you both up to the final leaf, together!"

The girls couldn't believe it. More beginner's luck! "Oh, thank you, bluebird!" Emily whispered.

She looked at Aisha in delight. "We're going to win!"

Chapter Seven
Sneaky Selena!

"Bluebird?" Emily asked the silver-crested bluebird. "Please would you ask the caterpillar to take us to the final space?" They were so close to winning she could feel it. They'd defeat Selena and the Games could go ahead as planned. "We just have—"

"Wait!" Aisha said. "I think this might count as cheating."

Emily looked doubtful. "Yes, but … If we can reach the final space, we could quickly grab the trophy. It wouldn't matter how we got it."

Aisha realised what was happening. "*No!*" she said. "It's the locket, don't you see? It's making us want to cheat. We mustn't!"

Emily felt disappointed, but she knew Aisha was right. She turned to the bluebird. "You're so sweet and kind, but we must say *no, thank you*."

The bluebird's feathers fluffed up and faded from blue to silver. Her eyes blazed purple, and she grew and grew. Two legs

became four, and with a crash of thunder
and a flash of lightning, the bird turned
into – Selena!

"You foolish girls," she said. "I nearly tempted you. Well, you're not having that trophy, because I'll get it myself!"

She flew towards the shining cup, but before she reached it, the butterflies left their places and created a fluttering, multi-coloured wall in front of her.

Selena pointed her horn at the butterflies and sent out lightning bolts. But the nimble butterflies dodged the lightning and gathered together again to stop Selena passing through their wall.

Grubb called from his tree, "Oh come on, will you?! I'm getting bored waiting up here!"

Emily shouted back, "But you're winning. Aren't you enjoying it?"

"No," grumbled the ogre. "It's not exciting at all. I thought cheating would be exciting, but it's just boring. I'm winning but it's not fun."

"It's no fun for us, either," said Aisha. "It's not a proper game when one player does whatever they like."

Grubb thought for a moment, then said, "If I stop cheating, will you put down your four-leaf clovers? Then we'll be even."

"No!" screamed Selena. Lightning crackled all around her as she screeched at the ogre. "Cheat! You must cheat!"

The girls weren't sure what to do. "Can we trust Grubb?" Emily whispered.

Aisha shrugged. "He was going to beat

us anyway. We could make him promise."

"OK," said Emily. "Grubb? Do you promise to stop cheating if we get rid of our clovers?"

The ogre waggled his hairy little finger. "Pinky promise."

"OK, it's a deal," said Aisha. She and Emily dropped their clovers down to Buckle.

Aisha glanced up towards the trophy and counted leaves. "Emily, you need a six to reach the top," she said.

Emily felt her heart pounding as she rolled the die and she squeezed her eyes shut, too afraid to look.

"You've thrown a six!" cried Aisha.

"No!" shouted Grubb.

Emily grinned and snapped open her eyes. "Maybe we don't need beginner's luck after all!" she said.

She climbed six spaces, pulling herself up on to one leaf after another. On the final one she found a butterfly with crystal wings. Emily climbed on its back and up they flew.

Aisha cheered as Emily hooked one arm around the treetop and stretched up. She grabbed the trophy and peered inside.

There was the Sportsmanship locket, sparkling in the sunlight. Emily reached in and took it out.

She was overjoyed. "We did it!" she sang out.

Selena swooped towards her. "No!" she screamed.

But the butterflies made their rainbow wall and even though the unicorn tried to leap it, they were too quick. They blocked her way every time.

"Hooray!" cried Aisha. "We won!"

Buckle peered through the branches and gave a thumbs up. "Well done!" he called.

But Grubb's flabby ears drooped, and his bumpy, lumpy face looked sad. "I can't believe I lost my locket," he grumbled.

Selena swooped over to him, her eyes blazing. "It's not your locket," she screamed. "It's *mine*! Get back to my castle – NOW!"

Grubb looked utterly miserable as he clambered down from the tree and lumbered off into the distance.

The furious unicorn circled the thicket. "I still have one more locket," she snarled at the girls. "I'll make sure you *never* get it back. Not unless you make me queen!"

She soared into the air amid claps of thunder and crackling lightning bolts.

The butterfly with crystal wings

fluttered to Emily. "I'll take you to Buckle," she said in a tinkling voice. "You can't climb down with that huge trophy."

"What about Aisha?" Emily asked.

"I'm OK!" Aisha laughed. The caterpillars had joined up, end to end, to make a long pink and purple slide!

Emily's butterfly flew once around Flitter Thicket, to cheers from all the caterpillars and butterflies. With a "Wheee!" from Aisha, they were both down with Buckle.

"Well done," he said, grinning. "You did a grand job."

Aisha and Emily smiled happily.

The game board hovered in front of Buckle once more. As he took it in his

hands, light rushed towards it from every
direction. It tinted everything gold –
butterflies, trees, caterpillars, even Buckle's

top hat! The light gathered in the middle of the board and, as Buckle closed it, the golden glow disappeared. The girls' top hats lost their glow too as they rose into the air and vanished.

Aisha and Emily had done it! They'd won the game and got the locket back.

And they'd done it fairly.

Chapter Eight
A Joyful Flight

As the girls grinned and hugged each
other, more cheers sounded from behind
them.

"Hooray for Emily and Aisha!"

"They won! They won!"

The girls turned to see Hob, Ember and
Trixie riding on Fairtail's back as she flew

down to land beside them. Ember's six chicks were snuggled beneath her wings. "Emi-ly's the win-ner!" they chanted.

"You saved my Sportsmanship locket," said Fairtail. "Thank you."

Emily hung the locket around the unicorn's neck. Fairtail's horn sparkled and she tossed her head joyfully.

"Jump on my back, girls," she said. "Hob, too."

They said goodbye to Buckle and mounted the unicorn. Aisha sat with Hob in front and Emily behind as Fairtail soared high into the sky. Ember's chicks clung on to her mane, squealing with joy.

Trixie and Ember swooped around them. They were happy to stretch their wings at last!

"We're going to the stadium," the unicorn called.

As they flew, Emily spotted the young turtle, happily doing his homework. His mum sat quietly beside him, weaving a reed basket. Near the palace, Aisha pointed to where Billy the pufflebunny and Whiskerina the kitterfly were whizzing downhill on their go-karts, laughing happily.

"Your locket's working its magic, Fairtail," she yelled.

"I know!" the unicorn called back. "It's great to hear cheerful voices instead of squabbles!" She dodged a relay race between elves on flying scooters, and just missed the Bat Brigade zooming around a floating obstacle course.

Fairtail landed near where her unicorn friends were practising in the showjumping arena.

"Wow!" said Emily. "This showjumping is much more exciting than where we come from!" There were no fences at all on the course. Instead, as each unicorn cantered up to a flag, they performed elegant aerial stunts.

"It's like ballet in the air," sighed Aisha. "So beautiful."

Queen Aurora and the other Sports and Games Unicorns galloped over.

Emily and Aisha held the trophy

between them and lifted it high in the air. "We did it!" they cried.

"Thank you so much!" said Aurora. "You only have to look around to see how important it is for Fairtail to have her locket back."

Spiritmane asked anxiously, "You will help me find my Perseverance locket, won't you?"

"Of course," said Aisha. "We know the Enchanted Valley Games can't go ahead until you're wearing it again."

"It's time for us to leave now," added Emily. "But we promise to come back."

The girls threw their arms around Aurora's neck and hugged her, then said goodbye to their unicorn friends and their board game partners.

"I'll call for you soon," said the queen. "Watch those keyrings!"

Aisha smiled. "We will!"

Aurora pointed her golden horn towards the girls. Sparkles streamed from it and surrounded them. As they felt their feet leave the ground, the sparkles swirled into a whirl of colour and Enchanted Valley disappeared from sight.

"Bye!" they cried.

Moments later, the sparkles faded and the girls touched down on soft carpet. They were back in the living room of Enchanted Cottage.

Emily grinned. "After that adventure, I'm really looking forward to our afternoon's plans."

"So am I," said Aisha. "Let's have a board games tournament, with all our favourite games! Come on."

They poked their heads into the kitchen.

"Mum, Dad," said Aisha. "Please will you come and play a board games tournament with us?"

"Great idea," said Mrs Khan.

"I'll get some snacks and a jug of mango juice," said Mr Khan.

Soon, they were all sitting around the kitchen table with Aisha's Greedy Goat game board between them.

Mr Khan said, "Before we begin, there's a new rule. Dads get to start five spaces in front of everyone else."

Aisha and Emily burst out laughing. Then they each wagged a finger at him and said sternly, "No cheating!"

The End

Join Emily and Aisha
for more fun in ...

Spiritmane and the Hidden Magic

Read on for a sneak peek!

Emily loved school, but she couldn't wait for the weekend to begin. She looked out of the window and sighed. She wished she was already in the park, learning some new football moves from Aisha.

The clock on the classroom wall was almost at three. The second hand counted down. Five, four, three, two ...

Bringggg! Finally, the bell! Chairs scraped on the floor as everyone scrambled out of their seats.

"Have a lovely weekend, everyone, and don't forget your homework!" called Miss

Mayhew above the noise, as everyone stuffed their pencil cases into their bags.

Emily began to pack away … and then stopped. Where was her favourite pencil? The pink one with the unicorn at the end? It *always* sat at the top of her desk.

Read
Spiritmane and the Hidden Magic
**to find out what's in store
for Aisha and Emily!**

Also available

Book Nine:

Daisy Meadows

Unicorn Magic

Quickhoof and the Golden Cup

From the author of RAINBOW MAGIC

Book Ten:

Daisy Meadows

Unicorn Magic

Brightblaze Makes a Splash

From the author of RAINBOW MAGIC

Book Eleven:

Daisy Meadows

Unicorn Magic

Fairtail & the Perfect Puzzle

From the author of RAINBOW MAGIC

Book Twelve:

Daisy Meadows

Unicorn Magic

Spiritmane & the Hidden Magic

From the author of RAINBOW MAGIC

Unicorn Magic

Look out for the next book!

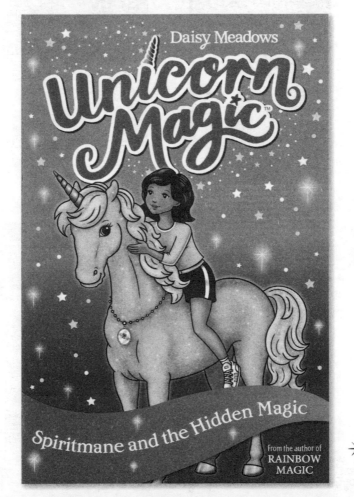

Daisy Meadows

Unicorn Magic™

Spiritmane and the Hidden Magic

From the author of RAINBOW MAGIC

Visit
orchardseriesbooks.co.uk
for

✶ fun activities ✶

✶ exclusive content ✶

✶ book extracts ✶

There's something for everyone!